Bed Pans, Chains and Ballroom Dance:

and Other Blind Date Horror Stories

Dr. K. J. Davis

Bed Pans, Chains and Ballroom Dance:
And Other Blind Date Horror Stories

For information address Wisdom Woods
www.thewisdomwoods.com
IBSN 978-1-952265-10-5
First edition, paperback, 2026.

This book is dedicated to my daughter, Tara, my pride and joy, who loves fiercely with her whole heart; to my granddaughters Scarlett and Ella – may you not have to kiss too many frogs to find a prince! And to the amazing strong women who came before me –
my Grandma Ella, Grandma Lil, Aunt Bernie and my mom, Lois
– I wouldn't be me without them!

Dear Readers,

This book is for anyone who has gone through some things in their personal life and has found themselves single (for whatever reason) and enduring blind dates from hell! I was that woman. I was married for nine years from 1987 to 1996, then divorced and living on my own for the first time (at age 32) with my 4 year old daughter. I had gone right from my parents' home, to college, then to living with my fiancé/husband. When I got settled in my apartment after divorcing I honestly felt like I could inhale and exhale deeply for the first time in a long time. I don't advocate divorce. But for me it was the right decision for a lot of reasons that I won't go into in this book. That's a story for another day.

After a while –however long that was– I found myself ready to enter the dating world for something to do during weekends when my daughter was with her dad.

That process started with well-meaning friends who wanted to "fix me up" with someone they thought was a great guy. Now keep in mind, these were people who were my FRIENDS and supposedly knew me well...or so I thought. Some of their choices made me question if they knew me at all or even liked me for that matter! And could they even SEE?! I know they meant well but they sure missed the mark! You'll understand after you read about Bachelor #1.

But first, here's a public service announcement: I'm aware that many men have dating horror stories about women who were bizarre on dates. But since I am female, I can only offer my opinion from that perspective. This is not a male bashing book because there are plenty of women with dating issues as well. We ALL have issues of some sort. The key is finding the person whose "crazy" compliments our own!

I am confident that the dates who did not work out for me went on to find great relationships with other people who were a better fit. I have no ill will, anger or resentment towards these men. Every experience was memorable and taught valuable life lessons

Oh...and just because...I added an inspirational quote at the end of each chapter because we all could use some positive motivation and food for thought. I hope this book can provide you with some laughter, along with hope for a 'happily ever after,' whatever that may be. Enjoy!

Kelly

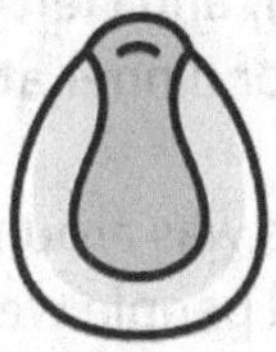

Bachelor #1: Bed Pan Man

A coworker's wife worked at a local hospital and knew a wonderful man who was a divorced surgical nurse with grown children. She thought we "would really hit it off." So, I gave her permission to give him my phone number. What would it hurt, right?

He lived relatively close by; only a half an hour away. He called me a week later and we chatted on the phone. Mostly pleasantries and basic information. He seemed kind, interesting and responsible based on what he shared about his career and parenting. He asked if I would like to go to dinner sometime, and I said, "Sure." We set up a date for two weeks later on a Friday night.

A couple days before the date, the gentleman called me to say that he had had some unexpected surgery and couldn't drive for a week. He still wanted to have our date and asked if I would consider coming to his house for dinner instead of meeting at a restaurant. His family had cooked a lot of homemade food for him, and he said it was delicious and there was plenty of it for us to enjoy. I felt sorry for him and gave him points for even considering keeping the date, given that he just had surgery. I didn't ask what kind of surgery. He said it was relatively minor, and I left it at that. I agreed to go to his house for dinner at 6:30 on Friday.

Keep in mind this was around the year 2000 when the world and people were considered safe in my naive brain. So don't judge me too harshly for keeping this date. Not in a million years would that happen in today's world if I was single.

I arrived at his house right on time that Friday evening. I didn't take anything for the meal because he had said on the phone that he had way too much food and there was no need. His home was out in the country; a one story modest house that looked harmless enough. And now the fun begins...

He opened the door and was a slightly balding man, small in stature with glasses. Okay, no big deal. Not Tom Selleck, but who is?! However, there was a large white bandage on the side of his neck, and he couldn't turn his head. Obviously, that's where he had surgery. Yikes! But I was still optimistic since he wanted to go through with the date.

He invited me in and we sat at the kitchen table. I asked him how he was feeling, and he proceeded to tell me all about the procedure on his neck. I mean graphic details that nurses rattle off like they're giving you an address and phone number. Bleh! I didn't need to know all that but he was a surgical nurse, so I took it with a grain of salt. My daughter is a nurse, so I have gotten used to graphic physical details of all kinds of things! He then told me that a lot of his friends and family had stopped by to see him and there were no more leftovers, so we were having pizza instead, if I didn't mind.

Okay, I love a good pizza. But this was no "good" pizza. He had baked a frozen pizza in the oven and served it to me on a paper plate, half cold. The center wasn't cooked all the way. And he poured me a glass of flat, warm root beer from a 2-liter bottle. He evidently was out of ice cubes too! What on earth!! This man thought this was an impressive way to serve a woman dinner on a first date?!

I endured the pathetic "dinner" making painful small talk. Small talk just sucks. There is no other way to say it. Meaningless chatter that is supposed to lead to something meaningful. However, this did not!

I was trying to think of ways to end the date quickly without being rude. I hadn't been on a date in 15 years, so my repertoire was beyond rusty. He asked if I wanted to watch a movie in his basement family room. I thought at least we wouldn't have to talk during a movie and maybe if I was lucky there would be microwave popcorn. Needless to say, the half cold pizza did not fill me up. I was still hungry!

So downstairs we went. And there it was! I looked to the left of the room and the ENTIRE WALL was filled with metal hospital bed pans! Yes, actual bed pans! Nailed to the wall on display. He began to tell me about EACH one. I wanted to pull my eyelashes out one at a time. How does one react to comments about bed pans?! In my case it was a combination of shock, disgust, and panic. I had to figure a way out of this situation, and quickly.

As he droned on, a visitor arrived who would later end up being my savior...a large fluffy white cat! Praise Jesus! We sat on the couch to start the movie; some action adventure flick. I've blocked it from my memory. And sadly, no popcorn was offered. Shocker! Every time he would go back upstairs to go to the bathroom or to get more warm root beer, I would fast forward the movie on the VCR. Yes, it was the days of the VCR! I had to get this over with and fast.

And then it hit me. I was allergic to cats (for real) and if I got an allergy attack, he would clearly see I needed to leave. So, while he was upstairs I petted the cat and touched my face. Hello sneezing and watery puffy eyes!! I was not above some temporary, self-induced discomfort to save me from this torturous date.

He noticed my symptoms and I told him it must have been from cat dander on the couch because of my allergy. I said I really needed to get home to take some medicine and use my eyedrops before it got worse. Thankfully, being a nurse, he understood my plight.

We walked upstairs and I got my coat and headed to the door. Now if I could get out of there without any physical contact with this man, I would be home free. I thanked him for dinner, and he leaned in to hug me. NOOOO! But just then I sneezed and backed the hell up right out the door! I apologized and bolted!

Once I was safely locked in my SUV and headed down the road, I realized how lucky I was to escape unscathed. Hungry with itchy eyes and nose, but unscathed. As I got further away, I got my cell phone out and called my best friend, Carol. I HAD to tell someone about what had just happened. I mean, seriously. WHO COLLECTS BED PANS?! And what are the odds that it's the first guy I have a date with since being single?! Then add in the bandage on the neck and the half-cooked pizza with warm root beer and you have a recipe for the worst first blind date ever. Well, not the worst. I wasn't hurt or kidnapped. My friend reminded me that going to his home probably wasn't the smartest plan, and that we needed to have communication before I went out on any more dates. So true! I needed her rational brain to snap me into reality.

When I went back to work on Monday, I made a beeline for my friend whose wife had arranged this little meet-n-greet. He was in shock about the whole experience, especially the bed pans. He apologized and said he would tell his wife to keep her dating ideas to herself going forward since obviously her radar was a tad bit skewed. I did learn from this outing not to go to a man's home on the first date, so it was at least beneficial in that way. Every life experience teaches us something - good or bad.

Food for thought: "Never be limited by other people's limited imaginations."

–Mae Jemison

Bachelor #2: Wallet Chain and Tires to Match

I didn't date for a bit after the bed pan collector, but a teacher on my staff took me aside one day and said she knew a "really nice single man" who she thought I would like. She worked at a car dealership on the side, so she met a lot of people. He had purchased a truck and other vehicles from that dealership, and she had known him for a few years. Being the eternal optimist, I agreed to meet him. She gave him my phone number and he called me a few days later.

He had a nice voice...calm, warm, and respectful. I got a good vibe from the conversation. We were set to go out for dinner at a local Mexican restaurant only a few miles from my house. He was going to pick me up on Saturday at 6:00. It was a date! While I had learned not to go to someone's house on a first date, I hadn't learned not to let someone come to my home and pick me up! It takes longer to teach an old dog new tricks, especially one who hasn't dated in a longgggg time!

Saturday came and I was in a new outfit. What is it about putting on a new outfit that makes you feel so much better?! It was just jeans and a new sweater...this date was in mid-November. But I was feeling confident and ready to take a chance on meeting a good man. The tick-tock of the clock was going oh so slow! Finally, I saw a truck pull up in front of my house. It was huge!! Like a truck on steroids. It was high off the ground and had silver pipes and all sorts of stuff that made it look like it should be in one of those monster truck shows or something. I took a deep breath and decided not to judge a book by its cover.

He walked up to my front door and there it was dangling on the side of his leg... a wallet chain thick enough to tow a car! Really? I've never understood those things. But maybe I've just never been in a position that requires my wallet to be chained to me?? Again, I decided not to judge until I knew more.

He was polite and walked me to the truck. But it was so high and I'm short, so getting in was going to be a challenge even with the running board. And let me add that my sidewalk and curb were covered in snow and ice. You guessed it... when I stepped up my other foot slipped, and I went down!

Excellent way to start a date. I was sore and embarrassed but not injured enough to cancel our dinner. I managed to get myself in the ginormous truck with his help. Good grief!

I have to admit I wasn't in the best mind frame for dinner at this point but I forced myself to carry on. We went for Mexican food, which is always a safe bet in my town. The conversation was so-so; not bad but not great. We mostly talked about pleasantries. I had leftovers to take home because the portions were huge.

I tackled the truck running board on my own this time and luckily made it unscathed. We pulled up in front of my house and he helped me out and walked me to the door. I was living in fear of the 'lean-in' for physical contact, but luckily my dog decided to come bounding out when I opened the door. Praise the Lord!

Then the strangest thing happened. He asked me if I was planning to eat my leftovers! Wait, WHAT?! He said that most people just take them home out of guilt and end up throwing them away. Okay, valid point, I guess. But then he asked if he could have my leftovers! What on earth is a person supposed to say to that?!! I mean, sure, here you go. I handed him my styrofoam container and backed him up towards the front door. I politely thanked him for dinner and said it was nice to meet him and quickly said I needed to get the leash to take the dog out in the back yard before he had an accident on the floor, which was the truth, sort of.

The lesson from this date was to never let a guy come to my house and pick me up for the first date. ALWAYS drive my own vehicle and meet at a safe public location so I could easily get away if necessary. Too bad I forgot this important lesson ON THE VERY NEXT BLIND DATE! UGH!

Food for Thought: "Success always demands a greater effort."

–Winston Churchill

Bachelor #3: Ballroom Dance

So those first two dates out of the gate were set-ups by friends. I decided I had enough of that and would try to go it alone and find someone myself. Online dating was becoming popular, so I thought I'd give it a whirl. What did I have to lose?! I didn't think I would encounter another person who collected bed pans or wore a wallet chain the size of Texas!

And at least I would be able to see a picture, get some background information and talk on the phone BEFORE going on the date. I figured online dating would be a much better option than a blind date. Right?

I took a leap of faith and created a profile on a popular site. I started out only paying for one month because I had no clue if this was going to be a successful endeavor. I can't remember what my profile caption was; "Looking for Mr. Right," "Still Believe He's Out There," or something to that effect. I started scrolling through various profiles that were a "match" for me. It was like going through a Sears catalog of men. Kind of fun!

Sometimes I would be looking at pictures with a drink in hand, making hilarious comments to the dog as I saved some and discarded others. It was an interesting way to kill an evening for sure. I ultimately decided that I would not communicate with more than two guys at one time. It was too much to keep track of, and I lived in fear of getting my conversations mixed up and saying the wrong thing to the wrong person. I learned that the hard way!

I started communicating regularly within the dating site with a man who lived about an hour away. He seemed interesting, charming, and polite. His picture was handsome; although it was only a head shot. I later learned to be leery of those and this experience will illustrate why. We eventually decided to exchange phone numbers and chat.

The conversation went well, and he asked if I would like to go to dinner. I need to add that one fact in his profile included that he drove a black Cadillac Escalade...my dream SUV at the time. I was such a sucker for a luxury SUV. STUPID in hindsight. But that was the reason I violated the lesson I should have learned about letting a guy pick me up at my home.

We set a date for Saturday in the afternoon. I decided that daylight was safer than evening for whatever reason. And I told my friend, Carol, that I was going on this date ahead of time since we were having lunch out of town. She was going to be available on her cell phone in case I needed to bail.

He rolled in my driveway around 1:00 pm in that beautiful black Escalade! I was watching through my sheer curtains in the dining room. Then he stepped out...a large man wearing black dress slacks, what appeared to be black dress shoes of some sort, AND a colorful shirt with parrots all over it. Last I knew, we weren't going to a Jimmy Buffet concert! I wanted to abort the mission right then and there. Could I pretend I wasn't home? No, my garage door was open and my car was there. Knowing my luck he would have called 9-1-1 or something anyway.

I had no choice but to answer the door and proceed with what I knew was a mistake. I could tell before he even got to the door. And for the record, he DID NOT look like his profile photo. NOT EVEN CLOSE! But I was committed and had to follow through at that point. How bad could it be, right? It was a daytime date and would be done in a couple hours. Maybe he would be an interesting conversationalist, at the least.

We got in his Escalade (which was one fine ride, I must say) and off we went towards Barnes & Noble. My initial thought was that I might buy a new book, which would not be all bad. We chit-chatted about various life facts and he brought up that he took ballroom dance classes, hence the black dance shoes. I knew there was something different about those shoes! But I had no idea why he wore them on an afternoon date to a bookstore! I asked him what his interest was in ballroom dance. Then the creepy part of this outing began!

He reached in the back seat and pulled out a photo album/scrapbook binder of sorts and plopped it on my lap. He told me to open it. Then he began to narrate all the photos and clippings as I turned pages. It was filled with things related to this female performer/dancer he followed. I mean, let's be honest. He was a STALKER of this woman! She was the reason he took ballroom dance lessons. He followed her career and went to MANY places where she performed. The last picture was of her jumping off a stage into his lap in the front row! He said that was the best day of his life.

I was literally speechless for an awkward moment. All I could manage to utter once I could speak was, "Wow, that's really something." Who has an album like this?! But even more odd, who brings it on a first date with another woman and then goes through it picture by picture?! In my head I knew I was going to need to call Carol and get the hell out of this date somehow. And fast! He was creeping me out! (I used way too many exclamation points in this paragraph but hopefully it conveys my level of emotion during this whole exchange. WTH!)

We arrived at the Barnes and Noble and I asked if he wanted to browse for books first before we sat down to have a light lunch and coffee. Let me add that I don't drink coffee but I would have faked my way through anything at this point in order for this nightmare to end!

As soon as he was heading to delve into a section, I told him I needed to use the restroom. I made a beeline to the last stall and pulled out my phone to call Carol. I spoke in an urgent whisper like a spy in the midst of a dangerous mission. I told her I was in the bathroom at Barnes & Noble and needed her to call me in 15 minutes and pretend to be my mom telling me that there was a medical emergency with my dad, and I needed to get to their house as soon as possible. The escape plan was in place!

I went out and found 'el creepo' and we sat down to review the menu board. And as luck would have it, my phone rang before we ordered! Go figure! The plan was activated. Luckily, I had a thespian background from high school and played the part of the worried daughter perfectly. Once I hung up I explained that he needed to get me back home so that I could pack up and drive to my parents' house; that my dad was not doing well and my mom would need my help. Lies, lies, lies! Lord, forgive me! But desperate times called for desperate measures. Let's not forget that this guy was a stalker in ballroom dance shoes with a parrot shirt on! No doubt God has forgiven me for this one.

We got back to my house in short order. On the way, I told him about all the health issues my parents had dealt with and how my brothers were just not as attentive and empathetic as me, and as the only girl a lot fell on me in times of need. All true! I wasn't a total liar. We pulled in the driveway and I hopped out and hurried to my front door. He kind of milled around and followed me, waiting in the foyer. Ummm...I explained I needed to pack up the dog and an overnight bag and hit the road. I thanked him for asking me out and apologized for the abrupt end of the date. Again, thespian skills. He just stayed there so I had to start to pack up. Evidently he was calling my bluff! Fine! Two could play this game.

I put my dog in his crate, grabbed his bag of food and bowls and sat him in the foyer. I grabbed my overnight bag from the hallway closet and quickly threw some clothes in it, along with my makeup bag. Honestly, I think it was all pajamas since they were in the same drawer. I lugged it all out to my car and loaded up. He followed me like a sullen puppy. It was creepy. I apologized again for the cancellation.

He tried to lean in for a hug or he was going to throw me in the trunk; one or the other. Oh, hell no! No stalker was going to put his hands on me! I quickly got in my car and put my seat belt on. As he was walking back to his SUV, I locked my car door. He backed out of my driveway into the street, then waited there for me to back out and drive ahead of him. Creepo! He followed me to see where I was going.

I had to think fast to get away from this guy! I called a friend of mine who lived a few miles outside of my town and asked if he and his wife were home. Thankfully, they were. I asked if I could come over for a little while with my dog, that I needed a safe place to hide to avoid a bad date, and that I would explain more when I got there.

He said to come on over, so I did. I ditched my follower through the traffic lights getting out of town. I think I actually ran a red light and he had to stop. Then I took some quick turns onto country roads. So I figured he would not know where I was heading, and he had to get on the highway if he was heading home. I felt like I was in an episode of Law & Order SVU. I carefully watched in my rearview mirror all the way to my friend's house. No stalker! Whew!

I shared my ridiculous adventure with my friend and his wife. He almost spit his dinner out of his mouth from laughing. It was the parrot shirt and the photo album of the lounge singer that put him over the edge. What are the odds?!

Who describes their obsession with another woman on a first date? OR EVER?! What was he hoping to achieve by doing that?

To this day, I have no clue. And furthermore, parrot shirts are only acceptable attire if you're going to a theme party, on an island vacation, or going to Jimmy Buffett's Margaritaville bar!

Food for Thought: "The secret of getting ahead is getting started."

–Sally Berger

Bachelor #4: Off to the Races- Giddy Up!

One might think that after a date with a stalker in a parrot shirt and ballroom dance shoes, a girl would give up on online dating. But nope! I didn't. My parents didn't raise me to give up that easily. And maybe, just maybe, it was a fluke and there really WERE some normal guys left in the dating pool. Whatever 'normal' means. Normal is in the eye of the beholder, just like beauty. It's unique to everyone. So back to my laptop I went.

My next encounter was with a gentleman further away...four hours! How on earth could this even be plausible?! But once we were having phone conversations, I couldn't help but want to meet him in person. He was smart, funny, sarcastic, and very interesting. We talked for hours at a time. And he was honest about having to use a cane due to a leg injury. I respected that, and I had to see if this could really go somewhere.

We decided to meet for a date. He really loved horse racing, so he suggested that we meet at the racetrack. I had never been to a horse race so that sounded like a fun date; cool fall evening, a couple drinks, some betting on fun horse names, learning about odds. What was not to like?! The evening was starting off great.

He actually looked like his profile picture. We already knew we liked each other, and the conversation was easy. The horse race setting was fun and exciting. He taught me about odds and betting. He shared all sorts of interesting information about race horses and trainers. It was fun. And the people watching at the track was top notch. There were ALL sorts of people at the races.

Then came the end of the night. Those are always tricky. If there's chemistry, physical contact is typically welcomed. If there isn't, not so much. But what if there is a perception of chemistry by one person but not the other? That is where the tricky part comes in. I knew I liked this guy. But I wasn't sure if he was vibing the same way about me. I thought he was, but not with 100% certainty.

He walked me to my car, leaned in for a sideways hug, and said he had a nice time. Hmmm... what was that? The side hug was something I deemed worthy of a cousin or relative you rarely saw or wanted to see. But there was the cane factor. Was it easier to hug sideways because of his leg injury and the cane? I didn't know. I wondered about it during my drive home. Would he call again? Or was it one and done? Was I wrong about the connection between us during all those lengthy phone calls?

He called me two days later and I welcomed it because I really did enjoy this man. But, to my surprise, he explained that the distance between us was too big a barrier for him. Well, he knew the distance before we met. Why did he even contact me or want to meet? Then he got to the real excuse; that he just wanted to be friends. Newsflash...people don't get on online dating sites to make friends. At least I didn't! I told him I didn't really need another male friend, and that I was looking for an actual relationship with a man.

So that was the end of that. I felt misled and strung along somewhat. This was the first time the rejection shoe was on the other foot and I was on the receiving end. It didn't feel so great. That was a good thing for me to experience though. I needed a humble reminder to always consider the other person's feelings whether you are the "dumper" or the "dumpee."

I wished him well and thanked him for some great conversations and put a period at the end of that sentence. I was appreciative of the horse racing experience. Watching and betting on the Kentucky Derby was much more pleasant after all I had learned, so it wasn't a total loss.

Food for Thought: "A woman is like a tea bag – you never know how strong she is until she gets in hot water."

–Eleanor Roosevelt

Bachelor #5: Work Release

I didn't go an any dates for a bit; a break was definitely needed. I was in the midst of basketball season anyway, which meant A LOT of games to attend and cover as a school administrator. That's how I met Bachelor #5. He was a basketball official, and I typically handed them their checks prior to the game.

This guy had done several games at my school and we chatted on a regular basis. He was decent looking, funny, and very personable. He was divorced, had no children, and lived in my vicinity. So, all good signs for someone worthy of a date.

He asked me if I wanted to grab a bite to eat after a game one night. We met at a local burger place. This was on a weeknight, which is not usually when I went on dates. But it went well; casual and no stress. The conversation was easy and we had a nice time.

So, there was a second date for pizza after the next game he was officiating at my school. Again, it was during the week. You will understand why this is important to note as this story progresses. As a single mom, I shared with him that I would prefer going out on a weekend when my daughter was at her dad's so I wasn't taking time away from our evening schedule and responsibilities during the week. He was respectful of that, and we scheduled a dinner and movie date for the next Saturday.

Saturday rolled around and he was supposed to pick me up at 5:00 for dinner and we were going to see a movie afterwards. Well, he called that afternoon and said he wasn't feeling well and needed a rain check. OK, fine. Things happen. But the background noise on the phone call didn't sound quite normal. But I didn't pursue it at that point. Mistake!

Another week went by and I didn't see or hear from him. That was odd. I was at the next basketball game and one of the other regular officials asked me where this gentleman was. I shared that I hadn't heard from him since he cancelled our last date. He said, "Oh, when was that supposed to be?"

I shared that we were supposed to go to dinner and a movie on the Saturday prior. He chuckled. I was perplexed by his reaction, and asked, "What's funny about that?" He replied, "A guy on work release can't really date on the weekends." WHAT?!

I was silent for a minute. I pulled that official off to the side during a timeout and demanded, "You need to give me more information on this guy and his circumstances. Is he in jail?" He affirmed that he was. "For what?" I asked. Evidently, he had a domestic violence charge for an incident that happened between him, his ex-wife and her new man. Sweet Mother of Pearl!! Why didn't he clue me into this fact sooner?! Now the background noise during the phone call made sense. He was in jail!

Needless, to say we never went out again. In fact, he stopped officiating basketball games at my school altogether. It was like he disappeared from the planet. I so badly wanted to call him and rake him over the coals for not being honest and up front from the start. But what good would that do?! Once a liar, always a liar, my mom would say. He was a liar by omission, and being on work release for a domestic violence charge is a pretty big thing to omit!

I never would have guessed in a million years that this guy was capable of domestic violence. He seemed so mild-mannered and kind. It just goes to show that you can never judge a book by its cover.

Food for Thought:
"All that glitters is not gold."
–William Shakespeare

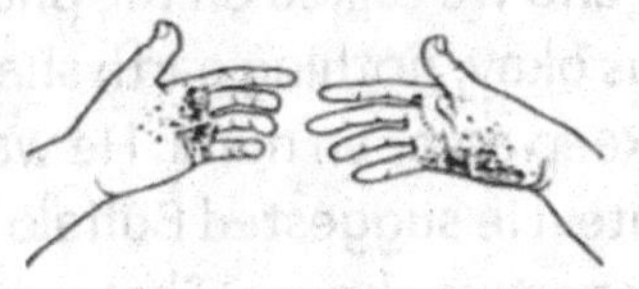

Bachelor #6: Cleanliness is Next to Godliness

After the setback of rejection and hurt feelings I got back on the horse, so to speak. I went back on the dating site in search of a worthwhile companion. I should note that whenever I was actively communicating with someone, I typically paused any other communications so I could focus solely on the person of interest. ("Person of interest" sounds like another episode of Law & Order. Can you tell I've watched way too many of those?!) Sometimes I would pause my online membership altogether if I was serious about pursuing a potential relationship.

So I was back to reviewing profiles and weeding them out. Back to initial emails and questions. Back to trying to discern tone, intent and meaning from the written word.

I started to chat with a guy who was somewhat interesting. I always tried to give people the benefit of the doubt because not everyone has effective writing skills. Some people are much better in person than on paper. I communicated with this new man for about two weeks. We emailed almost daily until he got up the nerve to ask if he could call me. He lived about half an hour from me.

He called and we talked on the phone. The conversation was okay, nothing earth shattering. But I wanted to keep an open mind. He was worthy of a lunch date. He suggested Buffalo Wild Wings which is very near my house. That was a bonus; if the date went awry I could easily get home quickly. We planned a Saturday lunch date.

I waited patiently in a booth at BWW's for him to arrive. I got there early because I wanted to pick the seating. I like to have a clear view of the door whenever I am out in public for safety reasons. I ordered a drink and an appetizer. At the least, I needed to eat something. He arrived right on time...blue plaid shirt and jeans. Okay, I could handle that. I like a casually dressed man.

The waitress brought some menus and we picked them up to browse the choices. And then I saw them...the dirtiest hands and fingernails I had ever seen! Eeewwww! What did this guy do for a living? We had not talked about details at that point. I knew he worked at a company that made some sort of ink product. But I had no idea he had his hands in the ink. And why would you not wash your hands and nails feverishly every day?

Maybe they were permanently stained. I didn't know. But I could not fathom those hands on my bare skin...EVER! It grossed me out. That may make me sound stuck up, but so be it. I knew what I could tolerate and what I couldn't.

It was like a train wreck...once I saw the hands

and nails I couldn't see or concentrate on anything else. I really do not remember anything from the conversation. It was uncomfortable and painfully boring. There was no connection for me. I don't think there was any spark for him either. I mean, if ink was part of your job wouldn't you find a way to get clean?

I remember my dad using a small pocket knife to get any dirt out from under his nails every night. He worked construction, so he was dirty when he got home each day. The first thing he did was take a shower and put clean clothes on before he ever came to the dinner table. He set the standard for what I expected of other men. He cared about his appearance. He worked hard and got downright dirty, but always looked nice when he went anywhere. I thought all men cared about themselves in the same way. Nope, sadly not true. No man could ever match how I felt about my dad anyway; who was I kidding?! I was his 'precious' and he was my hero.

The date ended and there was no misconception that there would be another date. We parted ways and went on with the day. Case closed. I learned that there are certain standards from which I will not waiver. Lack of cleanliness is a deal breaker for me.

Food for Thought: "It is our choices that show what we truly are, far more than our abilities."
–J.K. Rowling

Bachelor #7: Easy Rider

I waited quite awhile before I got back online again. I took time to just chill, read a lot of fiction novels, and had lunches and dinners with friends. I wasn't having much success in the dating world. But my career was on track and kept me very busy. And weekends were filled with cleaning, laundry, grocery shopping, doing some food prep for the week ahead, binge watching movies, etc. I have always been the kind of woman who was content to be in her own home alone.

The hectic pace of work life and working with the public made being home alone seem like a vacation. Being a hermit of sorts was just fine on MANY occasions. But eventually I logged back into my dormant online dating account and browsed who was out there. I was in search of someone new that I hadn't seen on the site for months on end. Enter bachelor #7.

Since the last guy, I decided that I would also find out details about someone's job before a first date. Not because I necessarily needed someone from a certain job classification; mainly because I wanted to avoid anything that was a deal breaker in terms of hygiene.

So, this next prospect met the criteria. He had his profession on his profile. We messaged each other on the dating site for a couple weeks before he asked for my phone number. One thing about this guy was that he was a pretty decent writer. I admired that. (I just had a random thought...I wonder how these blind dates think of ME; if they remember me at all?! They probably would have some choice words about me too lol.)

Once we got to know each other a little bit through our phone conversations, we decided to set up a lunch date at a local Mexican restaurant in the mall. No, not the same place I went with Bachelor #2. I vowed never to repeat locations where negative outcomes had resulted. We were planning on a 12:30 Saturday lunch; another blind date that was close to home so I could easily escape. He called me that morning and when I saw his number I was envisioning a cancellation coming my way. But he was just calling to say that since it was so nice out, he would be riding his motorcycle to our date. Okay, fine by me. It was insignificant. He could have been riding up on a horse for all I cared. Actually, the horse would have been more fun. I love animals. But I digress.

I arrived around noon so I could pick the seating location. You know my thoughts on location, location, location on a first date (booth with me facing the door). I ordered a drink and some chips/salsa. Then, my phone rang again. It was him. Okay, now he really was going to cancel. Nope. He called to say that he was IN THE EMERGENCY ROOM AT THE HOSPITAL. Wait, what? He had tipped over on his motorcycle and injured his leg and wrist and was in the ER.

Well, he was actually in the parking lot calling me because cell phones were not allowed in the ER, and he left the room against their policy to step outside and call me. I guess that earned some points. He said the nurses were yelling at him to come back in, and the call ended. I tried to call him later to check on his status but it went straight to voicemail. And I literally NEVER HEARD FROM HIM AGAIN!

I tried to call and email one more time to no avail. I was ghosted, or at least I think that's what it's called nowadays. I had no clue if he was ok or even alive. No clue why he didn't at least want to give me some closure. I was rejected and had no idea why. Honestly, that's probably the most frustrating kind of ending. I mean he could have at least given me the "It's not you, it's me" line or something. I had little to no emotional investment in this person; have the common decency and respect to tell me we weren't going to be going on any dates. If he's deceased, obviously he gets a pass. But my guess is since he could call me from the ER parking lot, his injuries were not life threatening.

Another reason this scenario did not work out was his name. (Not really, but I'm using that excuse to save face.) I have intentionally not included any names of individuals in this book out of respect for their privacy. But I'm making an exception here with a first name only. This guy's first name was Mel. I had a niece named Melody (God rest her sweet soul), and we all called her Mel. This was never going to work for that reason alone in my mind. My significant other could not have the same name as my niece; just wouldn't work.

In reflecting on what was learned from this guy…nothing profound comes to mind. Maybe to always expect the unexpected? That is the best I can do. Moving on…

Food for Thought:
"Gratitude is riches. Complaint is poverty."
–Doris Day

Bachelor #8:
Like a Crush on Your Best Friend's Brother

Did you ever have a crush on your best friend's brother back in junior high or high school? If you did, think back on it for a minute. It's worth reminiscing.

I'm starting this chapter with what I learned from this experience. First, you are never too old to have a crush on someone. Secondly, liking the sibling of a coworker/friend is VERY tricky because what if it doesn't work out? Will it impact the work environment and/or friendship? Luckily, in this instance it did not. But it is wise to tread very lightly and think carefully before engaging in a relationship with the sibling of someone you work with or are friends with. (As a former English teacher, I do not like ending sentences with prepositions and yet I just did it.)

I knew of this guy from all the times we were at the same party or bar because I was with his sister, who was a close coworker and friend. How I initially met him was because I needed some repairs done at my home. He did great work and we had good conversations whenever he was working at my house. I was like a lovesick schoolgirl on the inside whenever he was around. It was both annoying and exhilarating all at once. Annoying, in that I was old enough to know better than to get mixed up with my friend's brother. Exhilarating, because crushes are just such a rush of youthful exuberance. I couldn't tell if he was into me or just being nice because of my relationship with his sister.

One night we found ourselves at the same bar near closing time. Y'all know where that can lead. And as my dad always told me, "NOTHING good happens after midnight. EVER!"

Bottom line is after one brief 'date' I learned that he wasn't really into me and that I should never have gone down that road. But, to this day, his sister and I have never spoken about it. I'm not sure she ever even knew about it, which is evidence of his respect for privacy. And I still consider him a friend. He married a nice lady, and I moved on as well. So, all is well that ends well.

Food for thought: "Assumptions are the termites of relationships."

–Steve Sisgold

Bachelor #9: Another One...Really?

I took another hiatus from dating, but eventually jumped back on the band wagon of online matchmaking. I started communicating with another gentleman who lived about an hour away. He seemed pleasant enough. His profile was very direct, succinct, and no-nonsense. He worked in law enforcement at the prison near the town where he lived. This was a first for me; I had never dated an officer.

But I was optimistic because I assumed that a security guard would be someone who believed in law and order, rules, and structure, all of which I admired as a school administrator. My world was all about order, rules, and structure, and I had worked closely with the courts, the local police, and seen my fair share of juveniles who ended up going to school behind the fence (as I fondly referred to the juvenile detention center).

We moved into the phone conversation phase, and this guy had some interesting stories about his job. They topped mine ten-fold. That alone was worth a date. I was never bored in our conversations. So, we planned to meet near where he lived at a steakhouse chain restaurant. I was kind of excited about this date.

We both were divorced parents of teenagers; his were a bit older than my daughter. But we had that in common, in addition to the whole concept of keeping people in line at our jobs. Schools and law enforcement have so much in common in many instances, sadly.

I changed gears and agreed to a Saturday evening dinner this time. I had to change up my routine. The afternoon dates weren't going that well. But I did inform my friend Carol of where I was going, and our plan to abort the encounter was fully intact if necessary. I arrived early to hopefully select the seating, but he had beaten me to it. He also liked to sit in a booth facing an exit; must have been a police officer thing. So I didn't notice it until he stood up to use the restroom. There it was...a WALLET CHAIN!

Why, oh why?! Was this some male fashion statement about which I knew nothing?! Is it jewelry for men? Or is it simply to protect a wallet from falling out of the pocket? It was not as large as Bachelor #2's, but it was still significant. Strike 1! I deflated like a balloon slowly losing its air. What was it about those things that was unappealing to me? I think it might be because my dad was not a fan of jewelry for men. Beyond a wedding band and his watch, nothing else was acceptable.

The other issue which was more concerning was that when he stood up I realized he was barely as tall as me. Now I am a short person; only 5 ' 2".

That was also a deal breaker for me. My height or shorter was 'no bueno' for a mate! Strike 2! I can't even give a rational explanation for why that was such a turn-off, but it was. Another thing about all this dating was that I sure found out what I liked and didn't like, and what were deal breakers even if they were superficial, stupid and/or shallow.

Our conversation was average, but honestly I couldn't get past the wallet chain and height issues. Besides liking structure and rules, we didn't have as much in common as I thought we did from our phone conversations. Maybe everything was just tainted from strikes 1 and 2. Once I have my mind made up about someone, it's hard to change it. Personality flaw, for sure.

I knew we were headed for an awkward ending because he seemed to be falling all over himself to impress me. I was trying not to be harsh or dismissive, and focused on not hurting his feelings. Sometimes that felt like leading someone on or dragging out an inevitable ending.

He asked me if I wanted to go to his house for a cup of coffee and dessert; he had made a pie. That was sweet. And if I had been into him, I would have found it extremely charming. I felt obligated to at least try his pie since he had made the effort. His house was only five minutes from the restaurant. So, against my better judgment, I went.

The pie was actually delicious. And since I'm not a coffee drinker, he offered me a cup of tea. Again, very nice. But one of his kids unexpectedly came home and he awkwardly introduced me which I could tell he was not ready to do. That was totally okay because I understood that feeling. It was too soon.

The interruption was a welcomed one. It was the perfect opportunity for me to leave graciously, which I did. I thanked him for dinner and dessert. He said he would be in touch. Since his son was there, there was no risk of attempted physical contact which made my exit quick and painless.

Once in my SUV, I of course called my best friend Carol to update her of my date status. She always made me feel better, even when things had not gone well. Often, I felt like a subpar human being who was too brutal or judgmental or snobby. But Carol always provided the perspective I needed about dating. It was like trying on shoes. You might try on a lot of pairs until you get the right fit. It didn't mean that there was anything wrong with the shoes that weren't selected; they just weren't the right ones for you at that moment.

Yes! So true! I was as discerning about my choices in men as I was about the right pair of shoes. There was nothing wrong with that. I mean, after all, shouldn't we be selective about a person with whom we might spend our life?

The security guard did call me back two days later. I politely told him that I didn't think our relationship was going to work out for me. I can't remember how I actually said it, but I tried to be respectful and kind. He sounded so disappointed. He asked if it was because his son had come home. I reassured him that it wasn't that at all. I think I shared that it was just bad timing for me and my head wasn't in the right place to start anything.

These situations are so hard. There are only so many ways you can say, "I'm just not into you." That reminds me of the Sex and the City episode where Carrie's boyfriend, Jack Berger, tells her friend Miranda that if the guy didn't come up to her apartment after the date when she asked him to, that he just wasn't that into her. It was a shocking yet simplistic revelation. The women had been making it so difficult with all kinds of rationalizations that were complete bullshit. He just wasn't that into her! Plain and simple truth. Put a period at the end of the sentence and move on.

Food for Thought: "I restore myself when I'm alone. A career is born in public – talent in privacy."

–Marilyn Monroe

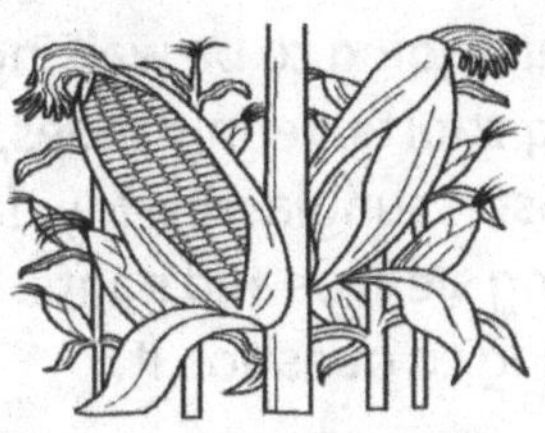

Bachelor #10: Corn Maze Mania

True to form, after an unsuccessful date, I took some time off from communicating with guys online. I think it was around this time that I started to binge watch episodes of Dateline. Man, there are a lot of men who kill their wives and girlfriends. Yikes! That show was getting to my head. But eventually I got bored with TV and decided to take another chance. So back to my computer I went.

This time I connected with a gentleman from Dundee, Michigan, about an hour away. The only reason I mention the location is that Dundee is known for its annual cornfield maze designs. That was what my online man suggested we do for our first date. It was September and that sounded like a fun idea. I hadn't been in a corn maze in decades! I checked the weather forecast and it was supposed to be a nice weekend.

Come Saturday it was a bright sunny day; a little too nice because it was going to be hot and humid. Those are two things I don't care for, but I was committed to the corn maze date. I drove to Dundee in what I thought was a good outfit choice based on the hot weather and the fact that we were going to be walking in a corn field maze; long shorts, tennis shoes, short-sleeved shirt, visor, sunglasses. My date, however, arrived in long sleeves and pants. Perplexing, but I wasn't going to question it.

Turns out, he was the wiser of the two of us. The corn stalks were ruthless and I had little scratches and cuts all over my arms and legs by the end of the adventure. That was due in part to the fact that we were LOST in that damn corn maze for an hour and a half! My date had the map but evidently didn't have the best map reading skills. There were people constantly passing us, going around us, yet he never asked which way to go. I wanted to step in and take over, but I got the feeling that he wanted to be in charge of the map, and that he thought he knew what he was doing. He told me that he had been to the maze before. Well, I certainly couldn't tell that by this outing!

I was a hot, sweaty mess with blood droplets scattered about my body. LOVELY! It was so hot in that maze with no air movement. Stifling hot. I felt like I couldn't catch my breath. What a miserable start to a date! I couldn't wait to get out of there and get to an air-conditioned restaurant so I could freshen up and have something of substance to eat with an ice-cold drink!

To my shock, my date had packed a surprise picnic and we were going to be eating outside on a blanket. Great! Normally, this might have been a welcomed endeavor but not given the hotter-than-hell corn maze debacle we had experienced. I endured the cheese, crackers, grapes, and cold cuts, and ate as quickly as possible so I could get back to my air-conditioned vehicle. I couldn't even fake how badly I wanted the whole date to end. When I am hot and sweaty, I am not a very pleasant person to be around. Just bein' honest. Then add in the abrasions from that corn maze and I was not a happy camper.

I thanked him for an unforgettable experience and for taking the time to put together a picnic. I said I wasn't feeling great, likely due to the heat. He understood and walked me to my car. I didn't even entertain any kind of good-bye hug. I wanted to be gone. I wanted to go home, take a shower to wash all the corn stalk residue and blood spots off, and get into my comfy bed. I checked corn maze off my bucket list. I doubt I will ever have the desire to visit one again...in my lifetime.

SIDE NOTE: To this day, I cannot remember this man's name, what he looked like, what he did for a living, etc. I think my brain just blocked it all from existence.

Food for Thought: "The best and most beautiful things in the world cannot be seen nor even touched, but just felt in the heart."

–Helen Keller

Bachelor #11: Possession is 9/10 of the Law

After recovering from the corn maze fiasco, I circled back to a guy online that I had been chatting with right before that date. He was still sending me messages and I thought he seemed pleasant.

But I found myself having serious doubts about ever finding anyone who was worthy of being a part of my life for any real length of time. I mean, was it me? I was second guessing my criteria, expectations, etc. for a datable guy. I remember talking to my mom about it. She always told me that people would be the biggest disappointment in my life, both personally and professionally. She wasn't wrong. My high expectations ended in disappointment MANY times in life. I need to add here that this guy only had head shot pictures on his online profile, so you know my hesitancy with this one and why I wasn't as optimistic as usual. While I still wanted to believe that people were honest and upfront, head shots indicated that they wanted to cover up everything below the neck. What were they hiding?! And why?!

Sadly, that was never truer than with this gentleman. He was HUGE! I'm not talking just some extra pounds or a beer belly. I mean VERY

LARGE! Now I've never been a skinny gal or interested in fat shaming people. There's fat; then there's obesity, and not the jacked up medical definitions of obesity. I couldn't force myself to be attracted to it. Some people are, but I am not. So, the cards were stacked against this guy right from the start. He had a handsome-ish face, so there was that in his favor.

During our conversations we had discovered that we had very similar tastes in music. So, for our date I took several of the CD's that we both really enjoyed. Yes, those were the days when CDs were still in use, and I had an extensive, varied collection; everything from jazz to country to pop to classic rock and a plethora of movie soundtracks. I was slightly addicted to movie soundtracks. Mostly from the romantic comedies that I was obsessed with, like Sleepless in Seattle, Runaway Bride, You've Got Mail, Pretty Woman, you get the idea.

(I have to interject where I'm at right now as I'm writing this chapter. I'm sitting at a Frisch's restaurant in my town in a booth having an iced tea and sandwich for lunch. Oddly, it's been a good place for me to write. But I am literally the youngest person here. I'm 61. Why is Frisch's the place for older people?! At least that is the case in my location. They have a fairly large menu, so I'm perplexed. Just my random observation. Back to the story.)

For our date, we met at a local restaurant/bar that was a popular watering hole for watching Saturday college football games. Safe choice, I thought. To my surprise, this guy was delightful. His personality was off the charts. He was both interesting and made me laugh. Plus, plus. It made the weight issue almost disappear. I genuinely was having a good time with him.

After lunch, we rode in his SUV over to a nearby metro park and sat with the windows down listening to some of the CDs I brought. We talked about music, movies, life, online dating, you name it. It was one of the best dates I had in awhile. He seemed to be having a good time as well.

When we were ending the date, he asked if he could borrow some of my CD's so he could listen to some music he hadn't heard in a long time. I said, "I guess that means we're going to have another date." To which he replied, "Absolutely! If you'll accept the offer."

I drove home feeling more optimistic than I expected, and more than I had in quite some time about the chemistry with this new man. It was such a pleasant surprise. He said he would call me when I got home from vacation. I was heading up north for a week on an annual trip to Canada. During that trip, I shared with my cousin about this date and the surprising experience I had with this guy. She could tell that I was somewhat smitten and very positive about where it could lead. I just couldn't believe how much this man's personality had won me over.

I got back the following Saturday and expected to hear my phone ringing or have a message on my answering machine. Yes, I had an actual answering machine at that time. My mother sarcastically named it "Mr. Man." If I was gone when she tried to call me, she'd leave the following message: "Well, hell, it's Mr. Man again. This is your mother. Call me when you get home!"

Sure enough, my machine was blinking. I had a message. But it was from my mother welcoming me home and telling me to call her, not from the new guy. Okay. Maybe he would call later or the next day; could be giving me some breathing room to unpack and get settled.

But Saturday night and Sunday passed with no call. Hmmm...should I call him? Nope. I decided to have patience and wait for him to be the one to initiate since he said he would. I guess it was also sort of a valuable test to gauge his level of follow-through.

I waited and waited. Days went by. No phone call. Then I realized he still had my CDs. Was that reason enough to call and see what was going on, if for no other reason than to give him my address so he could send my CDs back to me? I thought so! I called early in the evening. The call went straight to voicemail, so I hung up. I tried to call again later, closer to bedtime. Again, no answer and straight to voicemail. So, this time I left a simple message: "Hi M, it's Kelly. Just calling to see how you're doing. I'm back from vacation. If you want to get together, give me a call. Would love to see you again. If you don't want to, I can just give you the address to send my CDs back. Hope to hear from you. Thanks, bye."

Again, I waited several days and nothing. Maybe something had happened. A sudden illness, family emergency, you never know what life can throw at you, right?

I thought I would make one more attempt. I called and this time I heard, "The number you have reached is no longer in service." What? Was I being ghosted in the ultimate way? A phone number no longer in service? Not only was I disappointed on a personal level because I thought we got along so well. I got past that. BUT he still had my property...my CDS, dammit! How rude! I wanted them back. Should I drive to his house and force him to give them to me? I knew where he lived. But was it really worth it? I felt like I should just chalk it up to a lesson learned and move on. Clearly, either something had happened in his life, or he didn't want to pursue a relationship with me or BOTH.

So, I moved on. Afterall, they say possession is 9/10 of the law. I considered the CDs an undeserved gift. He would have to think about the fact that he took them from me every time he listened to them. Maybe that was a much-deserved guilt trip. Or maybe he threw them in the trash or gave them to someone else. At any rate, it was over. And I never gave anyone my CDs on a first date again, or any other possession for that matter. I also reminded myself, yet again, to never go on a date with someone who only showed a headshot on his profile. If someone was really putting himself out there in an honest way, he should show his whole self! Period!

> ***Food for Thought: "The most important thing in communication is hearing what isn't said."***
> ***–Peter Drucker***

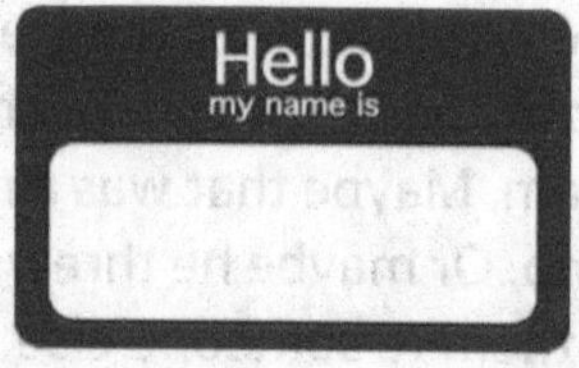

Bachelor #12: Three First Names

Despite another disappointing online dating experience, I had not given up on the possibility of a successful outcome. Was I a glutton for punishment? Maybe. I sure felt that way on more than one occasion throughout all these dating adventures. It often felt like the planets were aligned against me finding anyone who would be in my life in a real way, for any real length of time. Yet, as women, we often forge ahead anyway (men too). Hope is something that seems worth clinging to in matters of the heart. So back to the laptop I went.

I connected with another man who had the most pleasant face. He was an executive in a leadership capacity, so we had that in common. We had several good exchanges on the dating site and then decided to exchange numbers and talk.

He was delightful! He had a great sense of humor and we really clicked. The calls were frequent and fairly long. He was divorced and had two children. He was very involved in their lives and still had a positive relationship with his ex-wife, which I respected. All too often divorce wreaks havoc on the parental roles because the adults don't put their personal agendas and egos aside for the sake of the children. I was adamant that my daughter would never see or experience any animosity between her father and me. It meant biting my tongue a lot and sacrificing some of my own wants, but it was sooooo much better for her in the long run. But I digress...

This new man was like a breath of fresh air. He had realistic, full-body pictures on his profile, so I was praying that he was as he portrayed himself to be. We talked for about two more weeks before deciding to meet. We met halfway for a lunch date, and it went SO WELL! We had another date after that, and then he actually came to my office to see where I worked, and we went to dinner in my town. Things were going well. But here's the thing...which wasn't a big deal at all at the time...he had three first names; Mark Richard Allen (not really his name). Odd, right? It really wasn't significant, but unique more than anything. That is how I will always remember him; the guy with three first names.

We dated for about one month, then he got some sad news. His ex-wife had cancer. That is when everything changed. He became very involved in her day-to-day life again and helped with her care, and obviously more with his children. This was all very endearing. But there was little time in his life for anyone else, or at least he didn't make the time. It seemed as though he wanted to be with his ex-wife more and more, which I couldn't really complain about. She had cancer for cryin' out loud! Yet, it made our budding relationship next to impossible. It eventually was the reason we sadly decided to end it.

For the longest time that was the relationship about which I thought "what if" and "if only." I don't know what happened in their scenario. I genuinely hoped it would have a positive outcome for their family. He was a good man. It just wasn't in the cards for us.

Life happened, as it always does. This was a blind date over which I had no regrets. I felt blessed to have met the man with three first names. He restored my faith in the process, and in the fact that there were still good guys out there.

Food for Thought: "A pearl is a beautiful thing that is produced by an injured life. It is the tear that results from the injury of the oyster. The treasure of our being in this world is also produced by an injured life. If we had not been wounded, if we had not been injured, then we will not produce the pearl."

– Stephan A. Hoeller

Bachelor #13: The Angry Elf

This online dating match is the first that resulted in a somewhat long-term relationship that I considered serious. Looking back, I can't fathom how much I overlooked and how long I stayed with him. We were even engaged at one point! Thinking about it now makes me a tad bit sick to my stomach. But here's the story.

It was the usual emails within the dating site, then phone calls, then a first date. We met for dinner near where he lived. It was a nice date. We hit it off; he seemed polite, had a sense of humor, good work ethic, and liked the outdoors. At times, he seemed a bit stuck on himself and kind of like a bragger. I chalked it up to his trying to impress me on a first date. Number 1 thing overlooked.

In the first phases of relationships, it is so easy not to see fundamental personality flaws because we want things to work out so badly. The longer someone is single, and the more dating one does, the easier it gets to settle. But I'm shouting this from the roof tops...DO NOT SETTLE NO MATTER HOW LONG YOU ARE SINGLE!

He had very little baggage…only an ex-girlfriend who had a daughter with whom this guy still had a positive relationship. I wasn't concerned with either of them. Number 2 thing overlooked. This was not his biological daughter. Okay, but maybe they had a nice relationship, I thought. It was sweet that he cared about her. Or not. She called a lot and seemed to need a lot of attention and/or help. But I let it go.

I am not going to go into all the details of this relationship. Mostly because it is so unpleasant to recall and rehash, but also because it is embarrassing. I am an educated woman who, for lack of a better phrase, was a complete insecure idiot in this scenario! Luckily my mom and daughter saw this guy for who he really was and knocked me into reality.

We traveled a lot in the year we were together. He had a small motorhome, so we went camping and traveled to some nice places, including Key West and Siesta Key in Florida. I had never been a camping person, but it turned out to be an OK experience. I learned a lot. He also liked to go four wheeling on trails in northern Michigan, so he convinced me to do that as well.

That weekend trip was the first time I saw his ugly temper flair up. I had never driven a four-wheeler, and those were some serious trails. There were hills, trees, twists, and turns. I had a helmet on with a bandana and still felt like I was eating dirt the entire time. We were with some other couples, so there was no stopping. And the "angry elf" was not patient with me AT ALL! Number 3 thing overlooked. And this was a big one.

If your partner is not patient with you when you are doing something for the first time, DITCH THEM AND RUN! He was a total jerk to me in front of his friends, to the point that one of the other women took me aside and asked if we were having an argument or something. No, he was just a HUGE JERK!

Even now as I write about this, I am having a visceral reaction to the whole scene. I want to hurl every time I think about the time wasted with this guy and ever exposing my daughter to his toxic personality. He was a narcissist. And I don't think I knew what one was until long after this was over. But he could make me feel like his anger was justified because I was the problem. I was constantly second guessing myself. What the hell!

You might be asking how I ever got engaged to this person. I sill ask myself that to this day. The engagement happened fairly early...about 6 months in. It was almost like someone asking if you want to be exclusive; nothing romantic, no grand gesture. It was rather anti-climactic. Looking back on it, it was not without an ulterior motive. He wanted me to help fund a new motor home purchase, and figured I would never do that unless we were in a serious relationship with some sort of actual commitment. UGH! Luckily, the vehicle was not in my name. I paid for half of the monthly payment a few times and helped him find a storage facility for the winter. But that didn't last long because the relationship ended. So those few months of a payment were nothing in the long run, considering the bullet I dodged with this one.

How it ended was when I discovered that this guy was still talking to his ex-woman (who he had dated for over a decade) behind my back. Then it became not-so-much behind my back when he took a call from her when we were together one weekend, and hid in the bathroom to talk to her. What? Number 4 thing, but this time not overlooked.

I confronted him about it and somehow it was MY FAULT. Yep, his narcissism was on full display. It was an all-out war of an argument that resulted in driving home in silence. I was actually fearful for the first time that this guy might hit me. He didn't, but the fear was enough to shake me to my core.

We promptly broke up. I was relieved but also part of me was really upset. It wasn't because of losing him; it was the loss of hope in a life partner and frustration over all the time wasted. I remember crying on the phone to my mom and stupidly asking what was wrong with me. My mom shut that down and told me that it was the best thing to ever happen to me! She revealed that she and my daughter were planning to do an intervention with me to pull me out of the abyss if it didn't end. She was right, as usual.

There were still some remnants of this man at my house, and he wanted to come pick his things up. I was not feeling comfortable with him coming to my house and me being there alone. So, friend Carol came to the rescue as always. I had set up a time for the narcissist to pick up his things. I had them all neatly packed and boxed in my garage; it really wasn't much.

Carol was out there waiting for him. I stayed in the house. I need to add here that my best friend is fierce. She can handle anything that comes her way. I so admire that about her! And she can build just about anything. Behind the phrase, "Bring home the bacon and fry it up in the pan," should be her picture! So, the angry elf came to pick up his things. He made some snarky remark to Carol about me having her there instead of handling it myself, like I needed protection. That's right, jerk! I needed protection from the angry toxicity that was you!

I learned a lot from this negative experience.

Key takeaways were:

- Never ignore those things that don't feel right in your gut.
- Never settle for less than what you need or deserve in a mate.
- The most important relationship in life (second to that of faith) is the one you have with yourself.
- Narcissists are incapable of healthy relationships.
- Deceit is the gateway to the end of a couple.
- And here's the big one: IT TAKES A DAMN GOOD MAN TO BEAT NO MAN AT ALL!

Let that sink in.

Profound, isn't it?! I think Carol found this saying on a little wooden sign and gave it to me at one point. It was one of those times when I needed to be reminded that singlehood was sometimes the best road to be on. So true! The origin of this quote came from Dixie Carter's (Designing Women TV show) version, "It takes a mighty good man to be better than no man at all." If you are single and still searching for a life mate, embrace the place where you are right now. It can be a pretty great place if you let it be.

Food for Thought: "The more anger towards the past you carry in your heart, the less capable you are of loving in the present."

–Barbara De Angelis

Bachelor #14: How Nice is Too Nice?

After the narcissist, I hid my dating profile online. I was back to the point of re-evaluating my life choices and trying to "love the skin I was in" at that point. I had allowed that idiot to make me feel badly about myself and second guess myself. Let me say that again. I HAD ALLOWED HIM to make me feel like I was less than. Well, that was complete crap! Never again was I going down that road.

I turned all my energy towards being a mom and focusing on my job and the people in my life who actually cared about me. Not dating was refreshing, given what I had gone through. People at work were like my second family and filled a void in my life. I was content and healing from a period of relationship chaos. It had left a wide wake, and time off from men was needed; actually welcomed.

That was until a few months had passed and a colleague once again said he knew a "great guy" who would be worth checking out. This colleague was a local law enforcement officer who was a liaison in the school where I worked. I respected him and had known him for a long time. How could he steer me wrong?! Considering how much I thought of him, another blind date was worth a shot.

The man he wanted to fix me up with was divorced; had an ex who lived farrrrrrr away and two grown children who were out of the house. So far, so good. He also worked at a local factory and was an auxiliary police officer. Now, let's be honest. Who doesn't love a man in uniform?! So, I told him he could give him my number AFTER he showed me a picture of him that he had on his phone at a recent police function. I wasn't interested in a truly blind date. Salt-n-pepper hair, moustache, tall, muscular, kind blue eyes. Okay, what the heck. Count me in.

We had several phone calls before meeting at a local restaurant for dinner. He was the nicest guy I had met since the guy with three first names. He would be forever known as "Mr. Nice." Mr. Nice was so considerate, a good listener, caring and just plain kind. He was genuine and seemed to hang on my every word. I could tell he was smitten from the start.

He was the type who would call from work just to say "hi" and that he was thinking about me. He would drop off something simple like a bag of fresh sweetcorn for no reason. Mr. Nice was also a church goer who was not afraid to sing in front of a woman. He invited me to go to church with him. What you saw was what you got from him. WOW! What planet was this guy from?! I should have been in seventh heaven, right? Problem was, I wasn't.

He was TOO nice. Yes, I just said that. TOO NICE! (I have to insert here that my daughter will totally get this when she reads it. We are birds of a feather.)

As a strong independent woman who grew up with four older brothers who were construction workers, I needed a bit more of a challenge. Someone who would push back (verbally), be sarcastic, challenge my opinions or views, pick on me. Clearly, this was a flaw on my part because any other woman would have been blessed to have this guy. I tried to force myself to love him, I truly did. Because he certainly was on that path with me. But, sadly, I couldn't. There was no spark. Did I like him, yes. Was the spark there that I needed for love, no.

It was so hard, but I owed him honesty before this went too far. Even one month in, I knew he was going to be heartbroken. I had to end it; it was painful. I felt like a lowly scum. This literally was the epitome of, "It's not you, it's me." For real! I apologized so many times. He asked if there was something he could do differently to change my mind. UGH! Gut wrenching!

On Monday, I told my police officer colleague what had happened. I apologized for breaking his friend's heart. He said he understood; if the feeling wasn't mutual, it wasn't mutual. Guys were typically so much more levelheaded and matter of fact about these things than women. I had wrestled with it all weekend; felt like dirt. This time I really did ask myself what was wrong with me? Was I destined to remain alone? Maybe so. Only time would tell. I definitely had been through my fair share of dates and men at this juncture.

Food for Thought: "Without reflection, we go blindly on our way, creating more unintended consequences, and failing to achieve anything useful."

–Margaret Wheatley

Bachelor #15: Moth to the Flame

Head over heels. There is no other way to describe this one. It started on a weeknight on my 41st birthday in 2005. I was trolling the online dating site out of boredom and curiosity. A new feature of the online dating world at that time was being able to talk in real time within a pop-up-window; probably the precursor to face-timing. You could also see who was active online at that time and could message someone if you wanted to invite them to chat live.

As I was scrolling, suddenly there was a "ping" and an invitation from a guy asking if I wanted to chat? Wait, what? I had never done that before! Yikes! I nervously accepted the invitation, and there he was. We were talking live. It was surreal.

He lived only a few miles from me; what were the odds?! He was my age, divorced twice, with five children between the two marriages. And my balloon was deflating. RED FLAG, RED FLAG! But there was still something about him! I couldn't really describe it. Before the conversation ended, we set up a date for dinner Friday night at a chain restaurant; nothing fancy, just drinks and dinner at a local place.

Once again, I got a new outfit... dark jeans, a crisp white shirt, with a denim jacket, and clogs. Don't laugh. Yes, it was a spiffy outfit for a 40+ year old at that time. A new outfit always gave me an extra jolt of confidence. I wore my favorite perfume, Gloria Vanderbilt. I had serious butterflies and nerves about this one.

I drove to the restaurant and met him at the bar for a beer before we got seated for dinner. The conversation was easy and the beers were cold. Two hours flew by. We didn't really want the date to end. I knew that some of my friends were out for a night of beverages and karaoke at a watering hole in a nearby town. I asked him if he wanted to go over there to check it out. He did! He asked if I was OK with him driving us. I was. So, we walked to his vehicle...give you one guess what it was. A gorgeous new Cadillac Escalade! Oh man! This wasn't helping. You know my thoughts on that SUV. Yummy!

We went to that bar and when we walked in he put his hand on my back to guide me through the crowd to a table. It was like a lightning bolt hit me. He met my friends and fit in with ease. We had a great time! Closed the place down. I sang, we danced and just had an epic first date.

He drove me back to my SUV and the good night kiss was breathtaking. I was in dangerous territory with this one. I hadn't experienced this kind of chemistry in a long time. We ended the night with plans to see each other again.

I was with Carol the next day for shopping and dinner about an hour away from home. My phone rang and it was the new man; wanted to know what I was doing and did I want to see him again. Well, of course I did! But I explained that I was out of town with my friend. My stomach was doing flip-flops, like teenager kind of crap.

He called me when I got home and we made plans for the next weekend.

I was worthless the whole next week. I didn't know what end was up; what was happening to me?! I needed to get my head back on straight.

Well, I can tell you that my head was not on straight about this guy for a longgggg time. We were on-again, off-again for at least two years, maybe longer. We even went on a trip together. BUT, and this is a big 'but,' he never introduced me to his family or met mine. Most of his family was from far away so it was more easily explainable, but mine was only an hour away. Yet, there was always an excuse about why he couldn't make it.

WARNING! If someone you've been involved with for a decent length of time doesn't want to involve themselves fully in your life, then they aren't serious about REALLY being in your life in a committed way. End it. Period.

But is that what I did? Nope! That's where the quote from my mother comes in at the end of this chapter. I was being a doormat for this guy! He knew my feelings and was fully taking advantage of them, and I allowed it. I was being led by my heart with no regard that my head knew better.

Geography ended up being the only way the relationship ended for good. He actually moved across the world! Quit his job, left his kids, and moved. So bizarre and self-indulgent, in my opinion. To say he had commitment issues was an understatement; or so I thought. Eventually I heard he got married to a foreign woman and came back to the U.S. Evidently, he didn't have commitment issues. Maybe it was just the wrong time, wrong place, wrong person.

Everything happens for a reason. We have all been told that ad nauseam. It took a good long time for me to recover from this one and sift through what lessons were learned. The best I got from this was:

- Don't ignore red flags and your instincts for the sake of hormones.
- Genuine relationships involve being fully immersed in someone's life if they are long-term.
- Hot and cold men are no way to navigate a love life.

The best analogy for this one is the moth to the flame; eventually you get burned.

Food for Thought: "In order to be a doormat one must first lay down."

–Lois Davis (aka my mother)

This quote was often the precursor to a lecture about my choices. Oh, how I miss those lectures now!

*Bachelor #16: Don't #*it Where You Eat*

This is the shortest chapter in the book. I had a great working relationship and friendship with a colleague for several years. We got along at work and socialized together several times. We both had an affinity for cold Busch Light. At one point we decided to see if there could be something more than our current platonic relationship because we got along so well. My mother was elated because she really liked this guy! He was the salt of the earth.

But sadly, we tried dating, and it just didn't work. I was more into a romantic connection than he was. I was distraught for a little while and worried about the impact at work and on our friendship. But we both were mature and just went back to our old arrangement. It took some work and patience, but we still remain friends to this day and could have a beer together as if nothing ever changed between us. That's a testament to real friendship.

Trying to date someone where you work is another VERY tricky experiment that can be filled with land mines. Tread lightly, friends. The old adage, "Don't #*it where you eat" came to be for very good reasons. Enough said.

Food for Thought:
"True friendship is a plant of slow growth."
–George Washington

Bachelor #17: It's a New Day!

The song New Day by the Robbie Seay Band is the theme song of this final chapter. It's the song my last blind date played for me over the phone during one of our many calls. It's worth downloading if you have never heard of it. I have probably played it no less than 200 times over the years. If you need hope or reassurance that love is always possible, then you need this song in your life. So, I'll tell you how it happened; the happily ever after.

I went to a bachelorette party for one of my nieces on a Saturday night. I was 45 and still single. Actually I had been single for nearly 14 years and suffered quite a string of interesting dates and relationships, as you have read in this collection of stories. The last relationship did me in for quite awhile.

I hadn't been online in forever. My dating profile was hidden; maybe even deleted. I didn't really know. Or care, for that matter. I had all but given up on the online dating process. I figured I would have to magically bump into the man of my dreams in the produce section of the grocery store if it was ever meant to happen.

This bachelorette party was quite the soiree; lots of food, drinks, music and party favors at a popular island bar. But, seriously, how many plastic penis necklaces can a woman in her 40's tolerate?! I felt like a fish out of water but tried to embrace the experience following my mother's infamous words, "Do it with a happy heart!" If she said that to me once, she said it 1,000 times over the years. So, I played along because I truly did want to celebrate the upcoming marriage of one of my favorite relatives. But when I got hit on by some sleazy guy with a pick-up-line of, "Are you the sister of the bride?," that's where I drew the line and called it a night. I was just too old for this and had been through too much.

As I drove home, I played one of my mix CDs. You know those CDs we make when we are at a low point to punish ourselves with every sappy, romantic, lost-love song we've ever known? The clincher was "All By Myself" by Eric Carmen. That song could make a clown cry! "When I was young, I never needed anyone…all by myself, don't wanna be, all by myself anymore, all by myself, don't wanna live, all by myself anymore." I apologize because now that song is in your head. You may as well spend the $1.39 and buy it on iTunes. Man, I belted that one out with passion! But I didn't allow myself more than the ride home to wallow in self-pity.

Sunday came and it was a beautiful sunny day. I had plenty on my to-do list – laundry, planning my lunches for the work week, writing some notes about the tasks of the week ahead, going over my daughter's schedule – the usual. Yet, as I thought about the events of the night before, I decided I was going to make sure my profile was deleted from the dating site. Interestingly, it wasn't. I went through and deleted old 'winks' and messages I had never answered. I was ready to purge all my former attempts at connecting with men and move on.

Then, out of nowhere, came a wink and a message from someone new. I think his byline was "Just wonderin' what it would be like" or something similar. Great. Should I review his profile or just continue down my path of clearing out everything? Well, of course I caved and looked at the profile.

He was handsome, seemed genuine and straight forward; normal looking. I thought, "What the hell," and sent a 'wink' back. I didn't have a paid subscription anymore so I couldn't reply with an actual message. He responded again! Dang it. If I wanted to continue this, I was going to have to pay for another month. I got sucked back in; exactly what I had not planned on. Yet, something nudged me to continue.

Within an hour we had emailed back and forth, and he admitted that he wasn't great with email and would much rather get to know someone by actually talking to them. I could tell by his messages that typing wasn't his forte. He asked for my phone number. A few minutes later he was ringing me up.

He was shockingly blunt but not in a rude way. He was divorced with a son about the same age as my daughter. The conversation was effortless and went on for a long time. At one point he was eating corn on the cob (in my ear) at his neighbor's house. He didn't want to end our conversation.

The rest of my Sunday was consumed with talking to this new man. He ended one of our calls by telling me to have a wonderful "Simpson cloud filled day." What? I had no clue what he was referring to. He had to explain that he was talking about the white puffy clouds at the start of the Simpson's cartoon show. Duh!

We covered so many topics over the phone that day my head was spinning. It sounds cliche, but I felt like I had known this guy for years. I couldn't sleep that night because my mind was racing, and I was high on adrenaline.

During the week ahead at work, it was hard to concentrate. We were texting during the day and having evening phone calls into the wee hours of the morning. We had our first disagreement about education over the phone. It was a debate between public and private or home education. Being a lifelong employee of the public school system, I brought a different perspective to the topic he hadn't considered. Luckily it was summer and there were very few people at the school where I worked, so my tired eyes and diminished focus went unnoticed.

An interesting thing that made our pairing seem unlikely on the surface was that he worked in the construction world, and I was very much from the educational realm. But remember, my whole family –dad and four brothers – worked in construction their entire lives. I knew that world well. I admired that world. My father was in leadership roles in that field and taught me so much. I was comfortable with this new man's career, more than he first thought.

I was once told by a male friend that I "was a man's woman." Since I was raised in a household of all boys, relationships with females were challenging for me. I was independent, strong-willed and spoke my mind. I could cuss with the best of them and had learned to flip the bird in the tree house when my brothers taught me at the age of five.

I didn't understand or appreciate the drama often experienced in female friendships. And this new guy seemed to have a great appreciation and understanding of that. He actually referred to me as "effervescent." He was smarter than the average bear, and I liked it! I was an English teacher when I started my career, so vocabulary was a real plus in my mind.

There was so much connection happening, we couldn't avoid getting together. We had to meet and go on an actual date. Saturday, August 1, 2009 it was set. And let me tell you that I was never so excited and nervous for a first date. I broke every rule from my dating past...he came to my house, came IN my house, I rode with him in HIS silver mini-van (yes, a used mini-van), and I invited him in after the date was over. But I need to back up for a minute. When he came in my house to pick me up, this man planted a kiss on me that left me trembling. AT THE START OF THE DATE; right out of the gate. What nerve he had!

Wait, one important little fact that I forgot to share that complicated matters was that he lived TWO HOURS AWAY in another state. Since I wasn't active on the dating site, I had not set the distance parameters, or he would have been filtered out. How on earth could this even work?! I wasn't sure I could handle a long-distance relationship. Until I met him, that is. Honestly, I think he could have been a plane ride away and somehow we would have still pursued it.

We headed out to dinner in a neighboring town. He was blasting the song, Somewhere in America by Survivor, and was singing loudly. This guy had no shame. He was shocked I had never heard it. And he grabbed my hand like it was second nature.

The first thing that struck me was his tan muscular forearms. Yep, I know it's strange. But wowza were those forearms unforgettable! I wasn't the only one who was attracted to them; my mom (of all people) used to like to pat his forearms.

We sat in a booth at a Mexican restaurant and ordered two Corona's. I was going to impress him and show him how to get the lime to go all the way to the bottom of the bottle and back up. But it backfired and beer sprayed all over him! Embarrassing. But he wiped it off and we laughed about it. At one point during the meal he got up and came to my side of the booth to sit next to me. I was taken aback by his forthrightness. Who did he think he was?! It was both shocking and endearing.

Our relationship progressed at lightning speed. Within a few weeks he invited me to come to his town for an annual festival and I stayed in a hotel for the weekend. We definitely were not letting the distance be a factor. Every day, every conversation, every date brought us closer. We started to go to church together.

Next, came introductions with our kids, then my parents. His parents were deceased. We went to meet my parents on a Saturday. We went to lunch at a local diner/ice cream place which was called the Whippy Dip a long time ago. It had changed owners and names several times, but my mom always called it the Whippy Dip.

She was ready to grill my new man with questions. As she always said, "Inquiring minds want to know." She promptly warned him that I was fiercely independent and had been single for a long time; that I didn't need a man to take care of me. She bluntly asked him why he was single and why he got divorced. He answered with brutal honesty. He had nothing to hide.

Then something unique happened. He was asking my mom about her marriage to my dad. She talked about how she had to be feisty, talk back and give dad every ounce of fight that he gave to her. My parents fought a lot during their 61 years together. We called them 'the bickersons'. My man was quiet and then simply asked, "Do you ever wonder how things would have been different if you hadn't chosen to fight back?" My mom was speechless for a minute. That was rare!! He had a knack for saying something so profound that it stopped you in your tracks.

Bottom line –my parents loved him. To quote my father's profane comment to my mom after we left, "That's the best *#cking one she's ever brought home!" My mom had noticed how different I was with this guy; she knew it was serious.

So, here's the timeline: met online in August of 2009, dated throughout 2009-10, engaged in 2010, married in May of 2011. And we've been happily married ever since! He got down on one knee one Sunday in the pew at the end of church service as everyone was leaving and asked, "Would you make me the happiest man on earth and marry me?"

Many doubted our unique relationship due to the two-hour distance between us. But we have navigated it for 14 years now. I had a career near my home, along with my daughter and grandchildren, so moving was not something I was ready to do, and he had a job and home he didn't want to leave. So we saw each other on the weekends.

Now that I'm retired, sometimes I go there for a couple days during the week as well. It works for us. We're not together 24/7 so we don't get tired of each other. Some people may raise an eyebrow over that, but so be it. What works for some won't work for others. At some point we will likely end up in one home. Time will tell. We have had challenges like any marriage with our kids, jobs, dealing with the loss of loved ones, accepting the changes that come with aging, etc. Yet, neither of us would change a thing!

We each found our soul mate at the age of 45.

Closing thoughts:

Here are my random reflections from my season of dating after divorce:

- Online dating CAN work.
- It is possible to find someone over the age of 40.
- A marriage doesn't have to be perfect to be good.
- Distance is just one factor; love can be worth it.
- Opposites do attract.
- Sometimes a woman might have to kiss A LOT of frogs before finding her Prince Charming.
- Never settle or give up on finding the relationship you want and deserve in life.

What others think of your relationship is not your business. Let that sink in. It's not your business! So don't concern yourself with those thoughts. Best of luck to all of you who have been through some tough times and are in search of something and/or someone better on the horizon. It's possible. But if you choose to stay single, there can be happiness on that path too.

There is life after divorce; sometimes better than you could ever imagine.

Thank you for buying and reading my first book. May God bless you all!

About the Author:

Dr. K.J. Davis is a retired educator and school administrator who lives in Northwest Ohio near her daughter, son-in-law and two beautiful grand-daughters.

She has been happily married to "Mr. Right," who she met online in 2009.

They married in 2011 and recently wrote a children's book series together titled, "The Lumberjack and the Professor."

It is based on their relationship and the fact that opposites do indeed attract.

She enjoys a quieter life of reading, writing, travel and babysitting grandchildren. Kelly is passionate about children and their education.

Part of her legacy is that one is never too old to learn or take a risk. She earned a doctorate degree at the age of 60.

List of Bachelors

Bachelor #1: Bed Pan Man
Bachelor #2: Wallet Chain and Tires to Match
Bachelor #3: Ballroom Dance
Bachelor #4: Off to the Races - Giddy-Up
Bachelor# 5: Work Release
Bachelor #6: Cleanliness is Next to Godliness
Bachelor #7: Easy Rider
Bachelor #8: Like a Crush on Your Best Friend's Brother
Bachelor #9: Another One...Really?
Bachelor #10: Corn Maze Mania
Bachelor #11: Possession is 9/10 of the Law
Bachelor #12: Three First Names
Bachelor #13: The Angry Elf
Bachelor #14: How Nice is Too Nice?
Bachelor #15: Moth to the Flame
Bachelor #16: Don't #*it Where You Eat
Bachelor #17: It's a New Day!

www.ingramcontent.com/pod-product-compliance
Lightning Source LLC
Chambersburg PA
CBHW012016050726
47590CB00009B/3206

* 9 7 8 1 9 5 2 2 6 5 1 0 5 *